The story of *Puss in Boots* has
been passed down for generations.
There are many versions of the story.
The following tale is a retelling of the
original version. While the story has
been cut for length and level, the basic
elements of the classic tale remain.

Once upon a time, there was a miller
who had three sons.

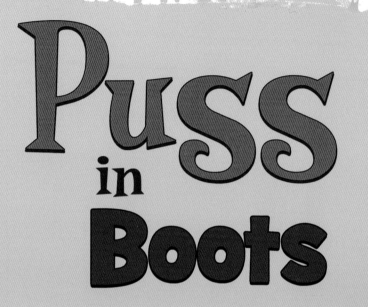

Puss
in
Boots

The Brothers Grimm fairy tale retold by Eric Blair
Illustrated by Todd Ouren

www.raintreepublishers.co.uk
Visit our website to find out
more information about
Raintree books.

To order:
☎ Phone 0845 6044371
🖹 Fax +44 (0) 1865 312263
🖳 Email myorders@raintreepublishers.co.uk

Customers from outside the UK please telephone +44 1865 312262

Raintree is an imprint of Capstone Global Library Limited,
a company incorporated in England and Wales having its registered office at 7 Pilgrim
Street, London, EC4V 6LB
– Registered company number: 6695582

First published by © Stone Arch Books in 2011
First published in the United Kingdom
in paperback in 2012
The moral rights of the proprietor have been asserted.

Art Director: Bob Lentz
Designer: Hilary Wacholz
Production Specialist: Michelle Biedschied
Editor: Catherine Veitch
Originated by Capstone Global Library Ltd
Printed and bound in China by Leo Paper Products Ltd

ISBN 978 1 406 22660 7
15 14 13 12 11
10 9 8 7 6 5 4 3 2 1

British Library Cataloguing in Publication Data
A full catalogue record for this book is available
from the British Library.

When the miller died, he left a flour mill, a donkey, and a cat to his sons.

The oldest son was given the mill. The second son had the donkey.

The youngest son was left with the cat, named Puss.

"What can I do with a cat?" he asked.

To the young man's surprise, Puss spoke.

"Bring me a bag and a pair of boots. I'll
show you what I can do."

The young man did as Puss asked.

Puss went off to a rabbit hole. He put his bag in front of the rabbit hole.

Soon a rabbit came out of the hole
and crawled into the bag. Puss quickly
snapped the bag shut.

Then Puss headed to the palace.

"I have a gift for the king," he said.

"Your Majesty, the Marquis of Carabas told me to bring you this rabbit," Puss said.

But there was no Marquis of Carabas. Puss had made up the name to impress the king.

Next, Puss trapped some birds. He went back to the palace and gave the birds to the king.

The king was very happy. He ordered a meal for Puss.

One day, the king and his daughter were travelling by the river.

"Do as I tell you," Puss said to the miller's son. "Jump in the river, and your fortune will be made."

When the king and his daughter drove
by, Puss cried, "Help! My master, the
Marquis of Carabas, is drowning!"

The king's guards saved the marquis.

The king told his guards to bring the
marquis a nice suit.

Puss marched ahead. He passed some workers in a field.

"Tell the king this field belongs to the Marquis of Carabas. If you don't, you will be killed."

The workers told the king the field
belonged to the Marquis of Carabas.

In the next field, workers were harvesting wheat.

"Tell the king this wheat belongs to the Marquis of Carabas. If you don't, you will be killed!" Puss said.

Finally, Puss came to the ogre's castle. The ogre owned all the land through which the king had passed.

"People say you can change yourself into any animal you want," Puss said.

"It's true," said the ogre. Then he changed into a lion.

"But they say you can take the shape of a mouse," Puss said. "Surely that is impossible?"

"I'll show you!" cried the ogre.

The ogre changed himself into a mouse, which Puss quickly ate.

The king arrived at the castle.

"Welcome to the marquis's castle," Puss said.

Everyone ate a delicious feast.

Finally, the king said, "Marquis, I would be very happy if you would marry my daughter."

The miller's son and the princess were married that very day.

And Puss became a great lord. He never again chased mice, except for fun.